Max Mouse is always looking for adventure. He is lively and full of exciting ideas.

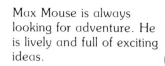

Joe Crow runs the airport in Fabuland. He is a fearless pilot, always ready to try out new daredevil flying stunts.

Wilfred Walrus is captain of the ferry, and loves to tell stories of life at sea.

Lionel Lion is the mayor of Fabuland. He feels very important as he drives round in his big shiny car.

written by
Michael Cole

Have you heard of Fabuland?
It's not far away – just a little to
the left as you go north, or a little
to the right as you go south.

Edward Elephant lives there,
and so do all his friends. Read about their
exciting adventures in this series.

Acknowledgments
Film stills by FilmFair
Book designed by Nick Freestone

British Library Cataloguing in Publication Data
Cole, Michael, *1933-*
    Edward joins the band; Clive's kite. — (LEGO Group).
    I. Title
    823'.914 [J]   PZ7
    ISBN 0-7214-1083-9

First edition
Published by Ladybird Books Ltd Loughborough Leicestershire UK
Ladybird Books Inc Auburn Maine 04210 USA

Printed in England

Edward joins the band

Ladybird Books

Edward joins the band

Lionel Lion was having a tea party at the Town Hall, and he had invited Hannah, Edward, Max and Bonnie.

Just as they sat down to eat, Edward saw a picture on the wall of Lionel playing a trumpet.

"Do you still play, Lionel?" Edward asked.

"Haven't played for years," said Lionel. "We used to have a real band in Fabuland. Listen to this."

5

Lionel put on a record that the old Fabuland band had made many years ago.

"Oh, those were the days…" said Lionel proudly. "I played the trumpet, Joe Crow played the saxophone, Wilfred Walrus was on the drums, and Boris Bulldog played the accordion," said

Lionel. "Oh, what music we used to make!"

"Why did you stop playing?" asked Edward.

"Well, we're all too busy now," sighed Lionel.

"What's happened to all the instruments?" asked Max, eagerly.

"Oh, we packed them all away in the clock tower," said Lionel.

"Can we see them?" asked Bonnie.

"All right," laughed Lionel. "But watch your step as you climb the ladder."

Max and Bonnie leapt out of their seats and ran on ahead to the clock tower.

"Wait for me," puffed Edward.

"Race you to the top," said Max, when they reached the ladder. He went up first, then Bonnie and then Edward.

Suddenly the big clock started to make a strange noise. Springs and cogs went whizzing round.

"Sorry!" said Edward. "I must have given the clock a knock. My trunk got in the way."

When they reached the attic they found lots of boxes.

"Do be careful up there," called Hannah from the bottom of the ladder.

They brought the boxes down the ladder one by one.

"Come on," said Bonnie. "Let's see what's inside."

There were drums for Max, a trumpet for Edward, and an accordion for Bonnie. There was a saxophone, too.

"Clive can play the saxophone," said Edward. "I'm sure he'll like it."

"We don't want Clive," said Max. "He always spoils things."

On the way home, Clive came to meet them. "Oh," he said when he saw the saxophone. "Lovely. Let me have a go!"

Edward was right. Clive *did* like it — and he was very good.

"This is fun!" said Clive.

When it was Edward's turn to play, his trunk got in the way and he made such a dreadful noise that it gave everyone a fright. He could be heard all over town.

Catherine Cat heard the noise in her kitchen, and it frightened her so much that she dropped a whole pile of plates.

"Oh, no!" she said.

Wilfred Walrus, who was dozing in his rocking chair, woke with a start. He thought it was the ferry's foghorn sounding.

"Hard to starboard!" he shouted.

15

And Lionel Lion was out driving in his car. When he heard the noise he thought that someone was hooting at him. He was so amazed that he nearly drove into a tree!

Everyone agreed that it would be better if Edward practised his trumpet out in the country — somewhere where he could make as much noise as he liked without frightening anyone.

They practised every day until, one afternoon, Hannah said, "Now listen, everyone! It's Lionel's birthday tomorrow and, as a special present, we're going to wake him up with some birthday music."

"I just hope Edward's playing has got better," said Clive.

Early next morning the new band met outside the Town Hall. Everyone took out their instruments – everyone, that is, except Edward.

"Come on, Edward," said Hannah. "We're waiting. Take your trumpet out."

"I don't need to," he said. "Listen!"

Everyone watched, and waited as Edward raised his trunk and blew, making wonderful trumpet sounds.

"You see," he said, "my trunk kept getting in the way but now I've learned to trumpet with it!"

"That's excellent!" said Hannah. "Now play along with us."

The new Fabuland band stood outside the Town Hall and played a special birthday tune for Lionel.

Lionel came out
onto the balcony,
smiling and
waving.

"Happy birthday!"
Hannah called.

"Thank you, thank you,"
laughed Lionel. "How good to hear
music in Fabuland again. It makes
me want to play, too."

"You can," said Edward. "Here's your old trumpet. I'm using my trunk."

So Lionel came down, took the trumpet, and led the band through the town, playing and singing out, "Good morning, Fabuland!"

23

Clive's kite

For days, the weather had been too bad to go out. Edward hated being stuck indoors, and so did his friends, Max and Bonnie. They were all miserable and cross.

Edward picked up a ball and started to play with it.

"Put that down!" said Max, snatching the ball back. "It's mine!"

"No, it's not!" said Edward, snatching it back again. "It's mine!"

"I had it first," argued Max.

"No, you didn't!" said Edward, and they both tugged at the ball, pushing and pulling each other round the room.

Just then Hannah walked past. She could hear Max and Edward quarrelling, and Bonnie shouting, "Stop it! Stop it!"

"Oh dear, what's going on?" said Hannah. She opened the door and went in.

"Now, now," said Hannah, "you mustn't let the weather get you down like this."

"But we're bored, and it's raining, and we can't go out," grumbled Max.

"I know something we can do," said Hannah. "We'll make some kites to fly when the sun comes out again.

"Edward, you fetch the paints. Max, we'll need some scissors and Bonnie, you bring the glue."

Hannah, Max and Bonnie settled down to make their kites.

"This is fun," said Max, dipping his brush into some yellow paint. "This yellow looks just like sunshine."

Then Edward came in with a big roll of paper. "Excuse me," he said. "This paper is very heavy." And he struggled across the floor, almost upsetting a paint pot over Max.

"Why don't you watch where you're going?" said Max.

"Oops, sorry!" said Edward. He rolled out the big piece of paper and started to make his kite.

Soon it stopped raining and they all set off to fly their kites.

Clive Crocodile came running to meet them.

"Can I fly a kite with you?" he asked.

"But you haven't got a kite, Clive," said Max.

"He can have a go with one of ours," said Edward.

"Yours perhaps… but not mine," said Max, holding onto his kite.

"Here, Clive," said Hannah, kindly. "You can use mine."

"Ooh, thank you!" said Clive.

"Flying kites is easy, when you know how. Pay attention, everyone. Look at me! First, you've got to throw it up…"

And they all let go of their kites, throwing them into the air.

The strings wound out faster and faster as the kites went up, high into the sky... Clive's with a dragon painted on it, Bonnie's with an eagle, Max's with a sun, and Edward's with a moon.

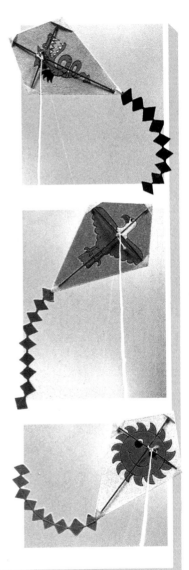

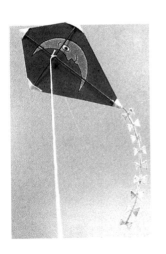

The kites seemed to dance in the wind and, as Clive's soared up above the others, he hopped up and down with excitement. "Mine's the highest! Mine's the highest!" he shouted.

"It's not a race, Clive," said Max.

"I know it's not a race, but *my* kite's the highest. My kite's the highest!" sang Clive.

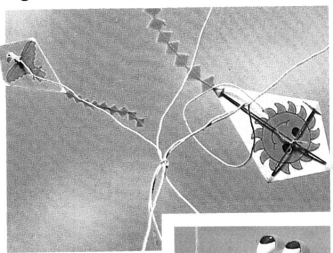

Then suddenly a gust of wind blew all the kites together and tangled them into one big knot.

"Come on, you silly kite," said Clive, pulling hard at his string.

"You mustn't pull on the strings, Clive," said Hannah. "It will only make the knot tighter."

But Clive wouldn't listen. He gave a big tug and broke all the kite strings.

The kites flew up into the air, riding on the wind until they were out of sight.

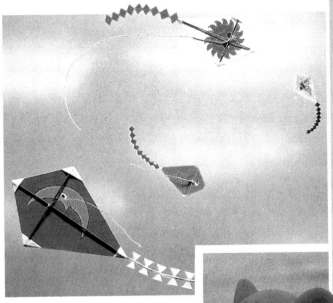

"Sorry," said Clive.

"Now that was a silly thing to do, Clive," said Hannah.

"Yes, it was," agreed Max.

"I've said I'm sorry," said Clive. "How many more times do I have to say it? I didn't mean it to happen. Sorry, sorry, SORRY!"

"Well, we can always make some more kites," sighed Hannah. "Come on, let's go home."

But when they got home they had a pleasant surprise. Three of the kites had come back. Only Clive's was missing.

"Ha! Ha!" laughed Clive. "Mine stayed up the longest. It went the highest and it's still up there! Mine went the highest! Mine went the highest!"

"Look out, Clive!" shouted Max, as a kite suddenly swooped down out of the sky towards him. But Clive didn't see it. He was too busy singing, "Mine stayed up the longest!"

The kite knocked him down, and a large bump grew on his head.

"Oh dear, Clive," said Bonnie, helping him back onto his feet.

"My kite *did* stay up the longest," said Clive, softly.

"And your bump will stay up even longer," laughed Max.

And even Clive had to laugh, too!

Freddy Fox enjoys running the General Store, and always has lots of bargains.

Mike Monkey spends most of his time with Wilfred on the ferry, although he should be helping Billy Bear to run the service station.

Poor Clive Crocodile is rather foolish and clumsy and he often spoils things for the others.

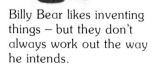

Billy Bear likes inventing things – but they don't always work out the way he intends.